Illustrated by DiCicco Studios, Casey Sanborn,
Warner McGee, and Kelly Grupczynski

Published by Phoenix International Publications, Inc.

8501 West Higgins Road, Suite 300, Chicago, Illinois 60631
Lower Ground Floor, 59 Gloucester Place, London W1U 8JJ

p i kids is a trademark of Phoenix International Publications, Inc.,
and is registered in the United States.
Look and Find is a trademark of
Phoenix International Publications, Inc.,
and is registered in the United States and Canada.

www.pikidsmedia.com

Printed in Canada

8 7 6 5 4 3 2 1

ISBN: 978-1-5037-1214-0

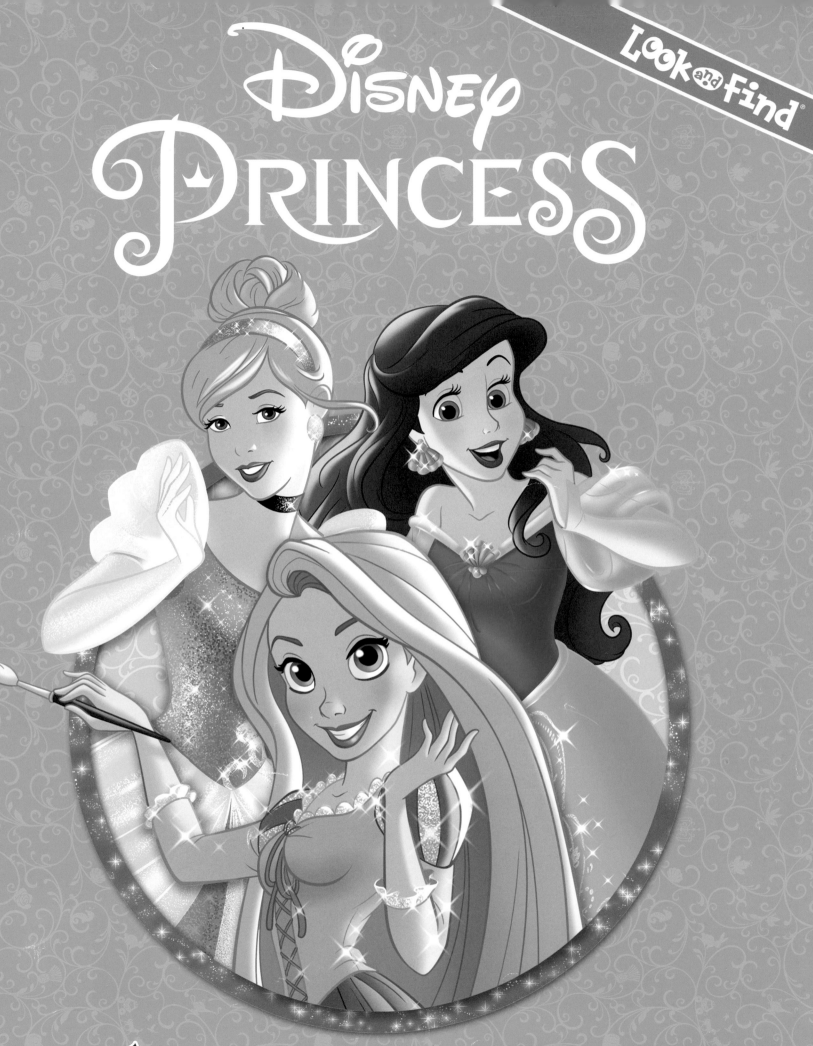

DISNEY
PRINCESS

phoenix international publications, inc.

Thanks to her little friends, Cinderella has a dress for the ball! Can you find all of these helpers?

Gus

this bluebird

Jaq

this mouse

this mouse

this bluebird

Belle loves to read!
The Beast's library is
filled with books she
is sure to enjoy. Look
around and find these
books for Belle:

*Sunny Days
Ahead*

Petal Power

*Friends of
Philippe*

Bird Words

*Dragon
Dramas*

*The Castle
Chronicles*

Painting, knitting,
dancing, reading...
Rapunzel has so many
ways to pass the time
in her tower! Look
for these things she
needs to be crafty:

palette

ballet
slippers

beads

knitting
needles
and yarn

glue jar

guitar

Ariel collects things from the human world as she dreams about life on dry land. Can you find these treasures from her collection?

dinglehopper

pipe

birdcage

violin

compass

boot

Snow White can always find time to sing and dance with the Seven Dwarfs. When you find each of these instruments, make its musical sound!

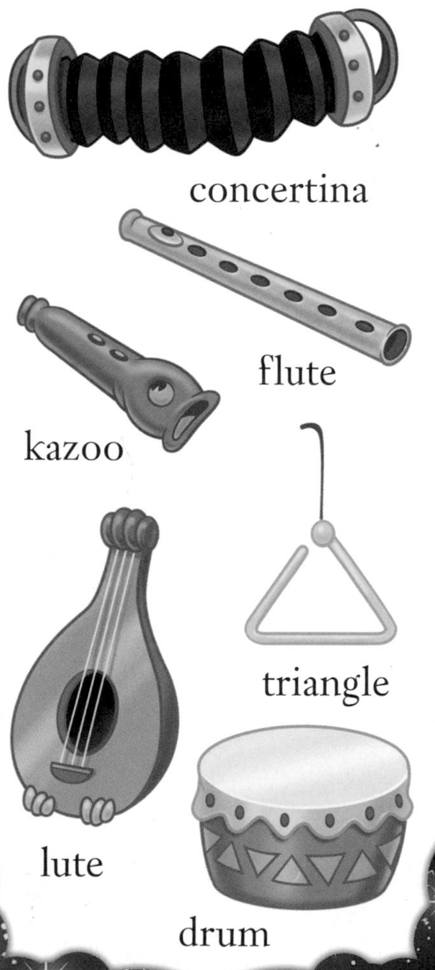

concertina

flute

kazoo

triangle

lute

drum

Everyone in Agrabah is living happily ever after... including Jasmine and Aladdin! Can you spot these happy faces?

child

baker

Genie

Abu

merchant

Rajah

Merida doesn't want to get married. And unless one of her suitors can beat her at archery, she won't have to! Can you find all of these arrows?

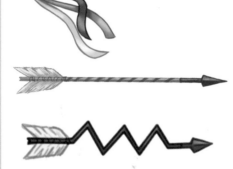

Mulan is a hero! She went to war and helped save her country. Can you find the friends who wish her a safe journey home to her family?

Cri-Kee

Chien-Po

Ling

Mushu

the Emperor

Little Brother

Cinderella's friends used lots of supplies to trim her pretty dress. Can you find and count each item below?

1 dress stand
2 baskets
3 pairs of scissors
4 red pincushions
5 pink ribbons
6 balls of yarn
7 spools of thread
8 pink bows
9 white buttons

Turn back to the Beast's library and look for all the letters of the alphabet.

Rapunzel stays busy with these big-and-little pairs. Return to the tower and see if you can find them all:

big sketchbook • little sketchbook
big feather pen • little feather pen
big paint jar • little paint jar
big ribbon • little ribbon
big vase • little vase
big doll • little doll

Ariel doesn't always know the real names of human things in her collection. She thinks a fork is a dinglehopper! Can you make up funny names for these treasures while you search for them under the sea?

toothbrush
necklace
clock
hat
book
plate

Colors help make Agrabah a happy place. Go back to the marketplace and find things that are:

red
orange
yellow
green
blue
purple
pink

"Arrow" rhymes with "sparrow," and "bow" rhymes with "go." Can you find these pairs of rhyming things around Merida's royal archery range?

crown – gown
bag – flag
ring – king
tree – bee
girl – curl
dog – log

In China, each new year is named after one of these **12** animal signs of the Chinese zodiac:

rat   ox
dragon   tiger
rabbit   snake
horse   goat
monkey   rooster
pig   dog

One zodiac animal is missing from Mulan's parade. Trot back and discover which one isn't on the scene!